Have you seen Elephant?

For
Mum, Dad
and Jo

Have you seen Elephant?

David Barrow

GECKO PRESS

Would you
like to play
hide and seek?

OK. You hide.

I must warn
you though.
I'm VERY good.

I'll try my best.

...10! Coming!
Ready or not!

Not under here.

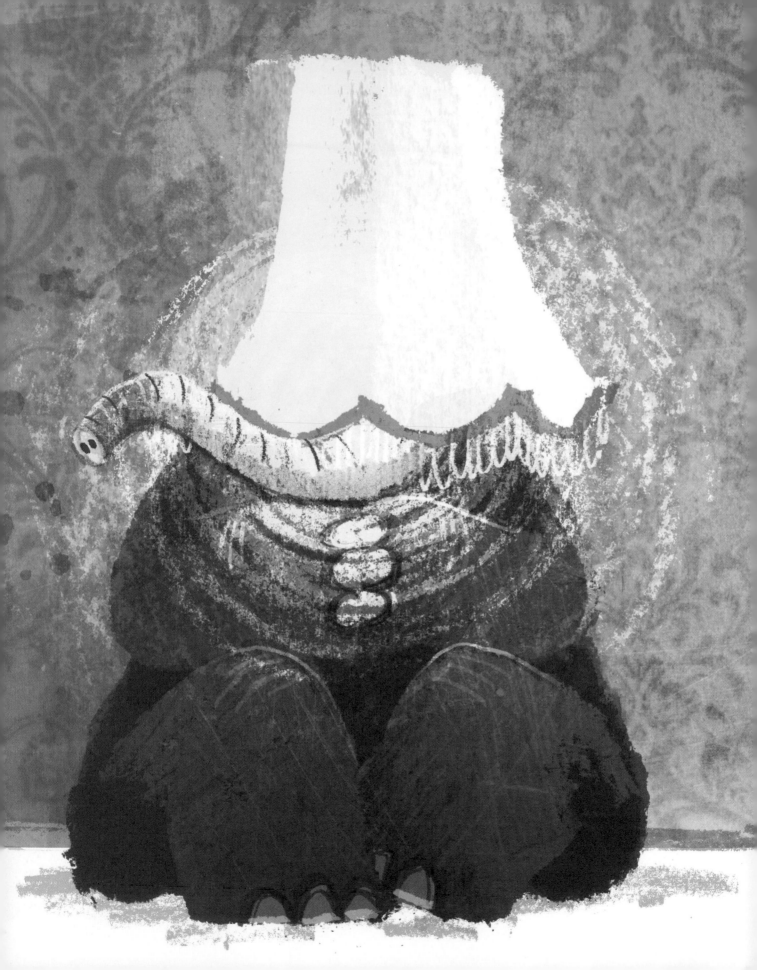

Maybe I'll try
outside.

I give up!

There you are!

Hey, what are you playing?
Hide and seek.

Would you like to play tag?
OK.

I must warn
you though...

... I'm VERY good!

First published in 2015 by Gecko Press
PO Box 9335, Wellington 6141, New Zealand
info@geckopress.com

This BookTrust edition published 2018

Designed by Vida & Luke Kelly, New Zealand
Printed in China by Everbest Printing Co. Ltd,
an accredited ISO 14001 & FSC certified printer

ISBN BookTrust edition: 978-1-776572-15-1
ISBN hardback: 978-1-776570-08-9
ISBN paperback: 978-1-776570-09-6
Ebook available

For more curiously good books, visit geckopress.com